JATAKA TALES SERIES

Great Gift
and the
Wish-Fulfilling Gem

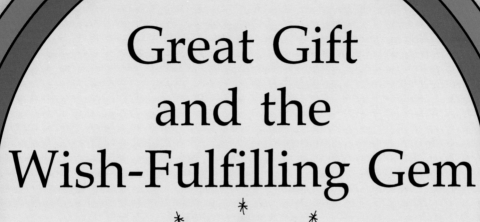

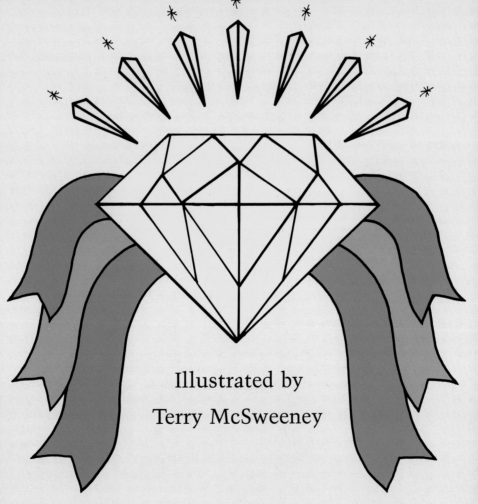

Illustrated by
Terry McSweeney

DHARMA PUBLISHING

Dedicated to all the world's children

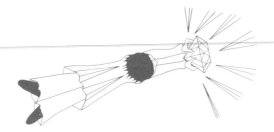

Endpapers by Margie Horton

Library of Congress Cataloging in Publication Data

Great Gift and the wish-fulfilling gem.

(Jataka tales series)
An adaptation from Lama Mipham's collection of
Jataka tales.

Summary: Great Gift, a good-hearted child of India,
seeks a wishfulfilling gem to correct all the ills of
the poor.

1. Jataka stories, English. [1. Jataka stories]
I. Mi-pham-rgya-mtsho, 'Jam-mgon 'Ju, 1846–1912.
II. McSweeney, Terry, ill. III. Series.
BQ1462E5G74   294.3'823   86–19767
ISBN 0–89800–157–9
ISBN 0–89800–143–9 (pbk.)

The Jataka Tales

The Jataka Tales celebrate the power of action motivated by compassion, love, wisdom, and kindness. They teach that all we think and do profoundly affects the quality of our lives. Selfish words and deeds bring suffering to us and to those around us. Selfless actions give rise to goodness of such power that its influence spreads in ever-widening circles, uplifting all forms of life.

The Jataka Tales, first related by the Buddha over two thousand years ago, bring to light his many lifetimes of positive action practiced for the sake of the world. As an embodiment of great compassion, the Awakened One reappears in many forms, in many times and places, to ease the suffering of living beings. Thus the Jataka stories are filled with heroes of all kinds, each demonstrating that compassion and wisdom have the power to transform any situation.

Although based on traditional accounts, the stories in the Jataka Tales Series have been adapted for the children of today. May these tales inspire the positive thoughts and actions that will sustain the heart of goodness and illuminate the wisdom of all spiritual traditions for the well-being of future generations.

Tarthang Tulku   *Founder, Dharma Publishing*

Long ago in India there lived the minister of a great king. Everyone paid him honor, for he was a kind and virtuous man, and rich as the god of wealth himself. The minister and his wife had a son named Great Gift, whom they dearly loved.

One day when the minister went to town he brought Great Gift with him for the first time. Seeing that many of the people were poor and had to steal or work like animals for their living, Great Gift became very unhappy.

At first, Great Gift wanted to give the poor people his family's riches. Then he thought, "Ordinary riches will not be enough. Only a wish-fulfilling gem could fill the needs of so many." That night he asked his parents for permission to search for a wish-fulfilling gem.

Now these marvellous jewels are guarded by powerful Nagas, dragons that dwell beneath the great lakes and oceans, or in far-away realms dangerous for human beings. Since his parents knew that no one had ever returned from such an impossible journey, they would not allow Great Gift to leave home.

For six days, Great Gift could not eat or sleep, thinking of the poor people he had seen. Finally his parents could not bear his suffering any longer, and agreed to let him go.

Soon afterward, Great Gift joined a caravan of five hundred merchants and set out to find the wondrous jewel.

After many adventures, Great Gift and the merchants reached the ocean, where they had carpenters build them a fleet of large boats. Then they set sail for an island known as the "Fountain of Jewels."

There they found the beaches and river-beds glittering with jewels, but none was a wish-fulfilling gem.

Great Gift helped the merchants fill large bags
with jewels and load them onto their ships.
When the ships were overflowing with treasure,
the merchants were very happy, and offered to
share them with Great Gift. But Great Gift was
determined to search further for the
wish-fulfilling gem. At the first shore they
reached, he bade the merchants goodbye and
went his way alone.

For seven days Great Gift walked through water up to his knees; then he walked seven days more in water up to his thighs, and another seven days in water up to his shoulders. Crossing a great mountain, he climbed down into a valley and came to a wide river. There his way was blocked by snakes coiled around the stem of a golden lotus, who hissed and spat poison at him.

Setting aside all fear, Great Gift sat down and
meditated on loving-kindness. Soon the snakes
felt the power of his love, and became very calm.
Bowing their heads, they allowed him to pass.

Great Gift came next to the land of the hairy man-eating cannibals. Smelling a human being, the cannibals rushed out to capture him. Once again Great Gift filled his heart with loving-kindness, and his love removed the cannibals' greed. They grew calm and gathered around him.

When Great Gift told the cannibals about his search for a wish-fulfilling gem, they were inspired to help him. Taking him on their backs, they flew four hundred miles through the air, and set him down in the land of the Nagas, guardians of the magical wish-fulfilling jewels.

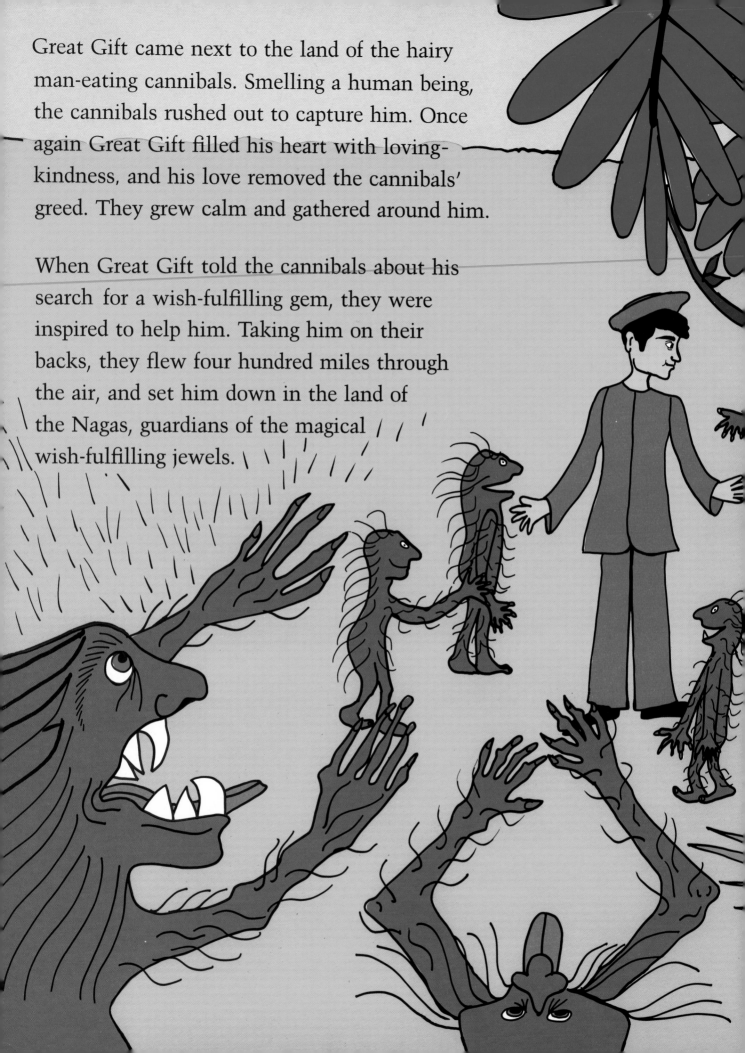

In the distance Great Gift saw a castle gleaming with
precious jewels. As he walked toward it, he found that
the castle was protected by rings of water filled with
poisonous snakes and guarded by two huge Nagas.

Great Gift's love calmed the anger
of even these fierce beings. The Nagas
lowered their heads, forming bridges
over the water with their bodies.
Walking on their heads, Great Gift
approached the jeweled castle.

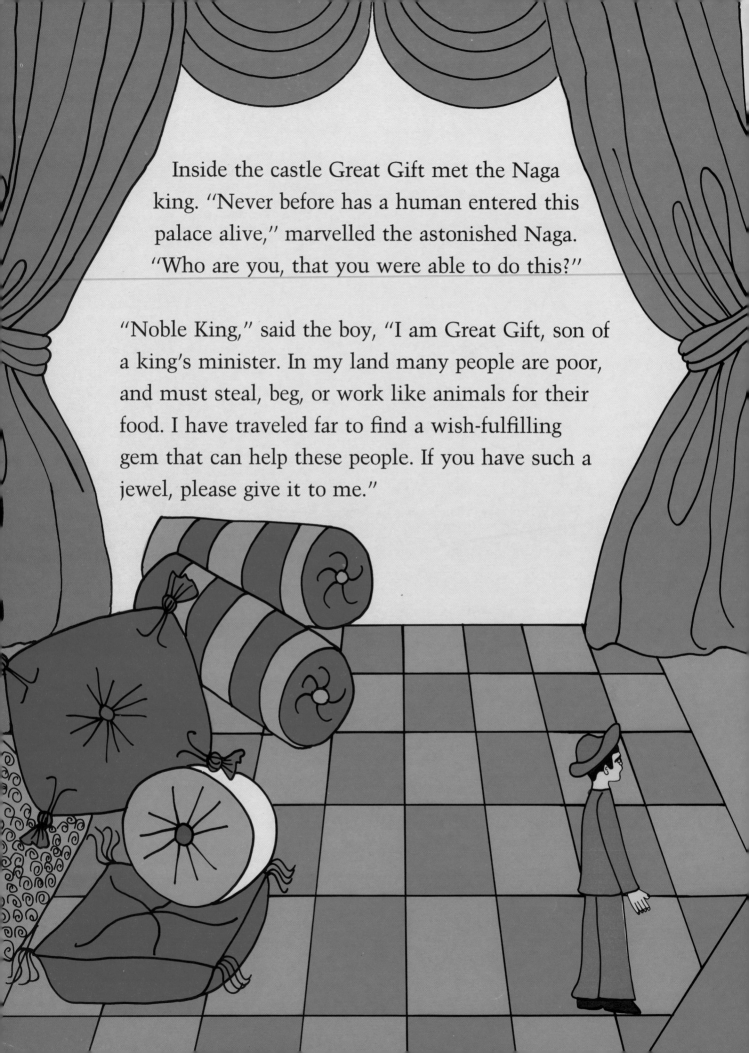

Inside the castle Great Gift met the Naga king. "Never before has a human entered this palace alive," marvelled the astonished Naga. "Who are you, that you were able to do this?"

"Noble King," said the boy, "I am Great Gift, son of a king's minister. In my land many people are poor, and must steal, beg, or work like animals for their food. I have traveled far to find a wish-fulfilling gem that can help these people. If you have such a jewel, please give it to me."

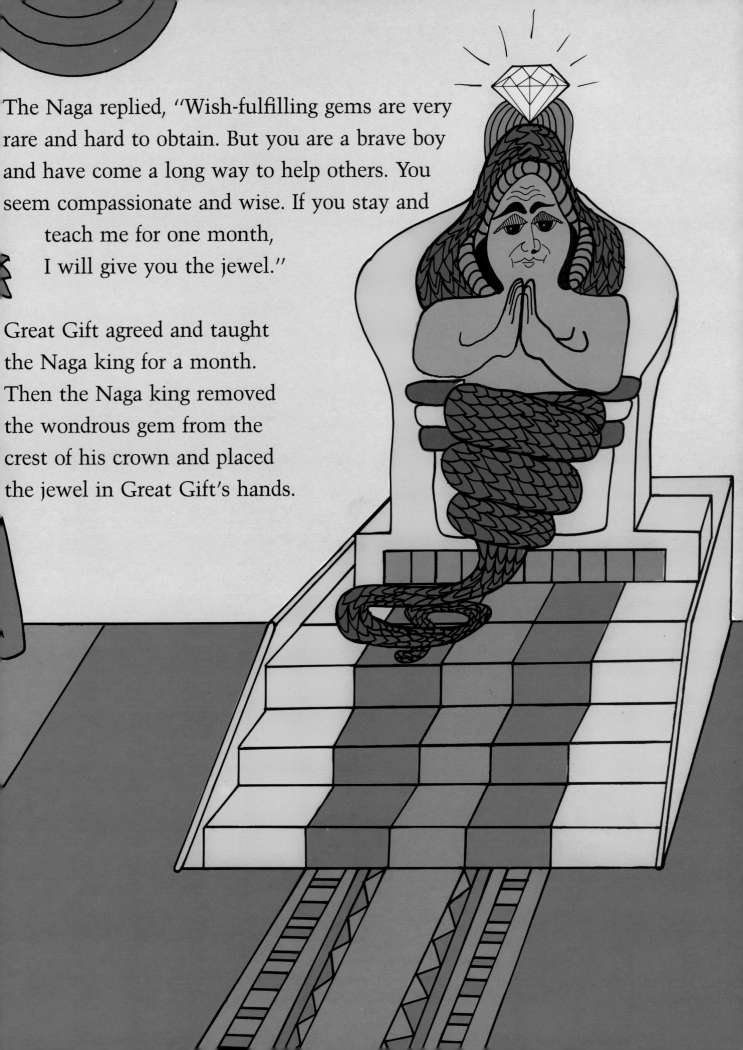

The Naga replied, "Wish-fulfilling gems are very rare and hard to obtain. But you are a brave boy and have come a long way to help others. You seem compassionate and wise. If you stay and teach me for one month, I will give you the jewel."

Great Gift agreed and taught the Naga king for a month. Then the Naga king removed the wondrous gem from the crest of his crown and placed the jewel in Great Gift's hands.

Raising the jewel above his head, Great Gift asked that it take him back to where his voyage began. Immediately he rose in the air and soared across the ocean. Then Great Gift made a second wish, and the jewel brought him home.

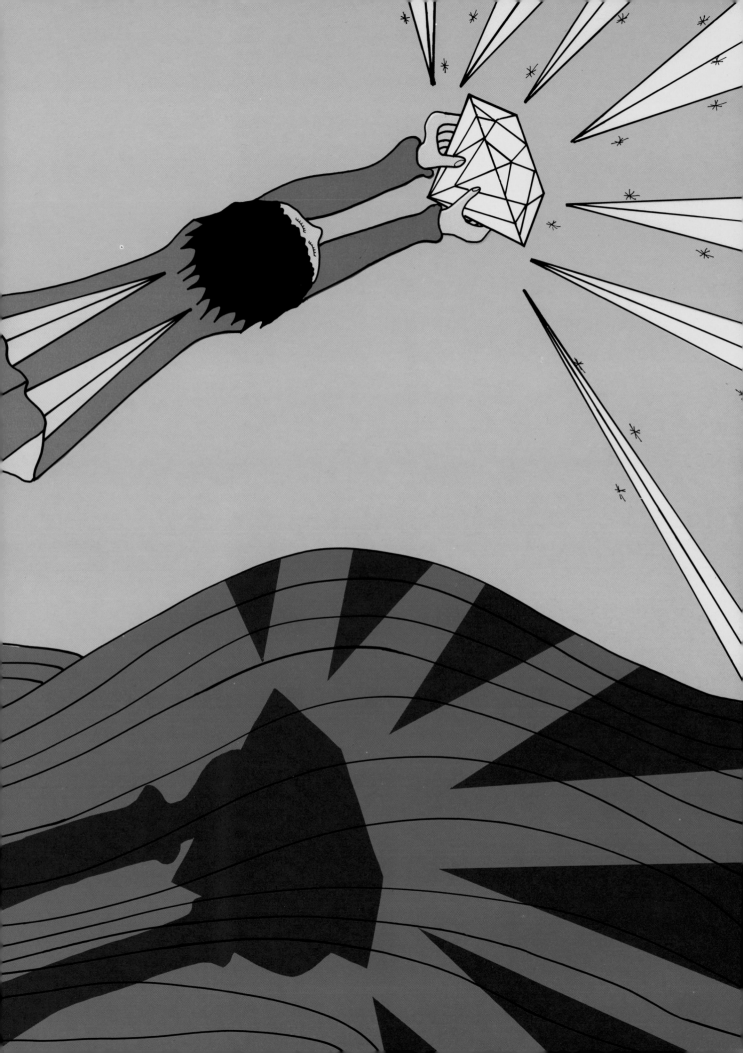

There he found that his parents, fearing their son was lost, had gone blind from grief. Lifting the jewel to their eyes, Great Gift restored their sight. His parents were overjoyed to see their child alive and well. "My son," asked his father, why did you risk your life for this particular jewel, when I already have such great wealth?"

"This jewel has great and wonderful powers,"
Great Gift answered. Then he lifted
the jewel again, saying,
"Many people are poor and unhappy. If this
is truly the wish-fulfilling gem, let it help
them now! Let there be a rain of everything
that will satisfy their hunger."

As he said these words, winds from the four directions swept over the land, then a sweet rain settled the dust. First there fell from the heavens many kinds of food; then there rained down grain, clothes, and jewels, enough to fulfill the needs of everyone on earth.

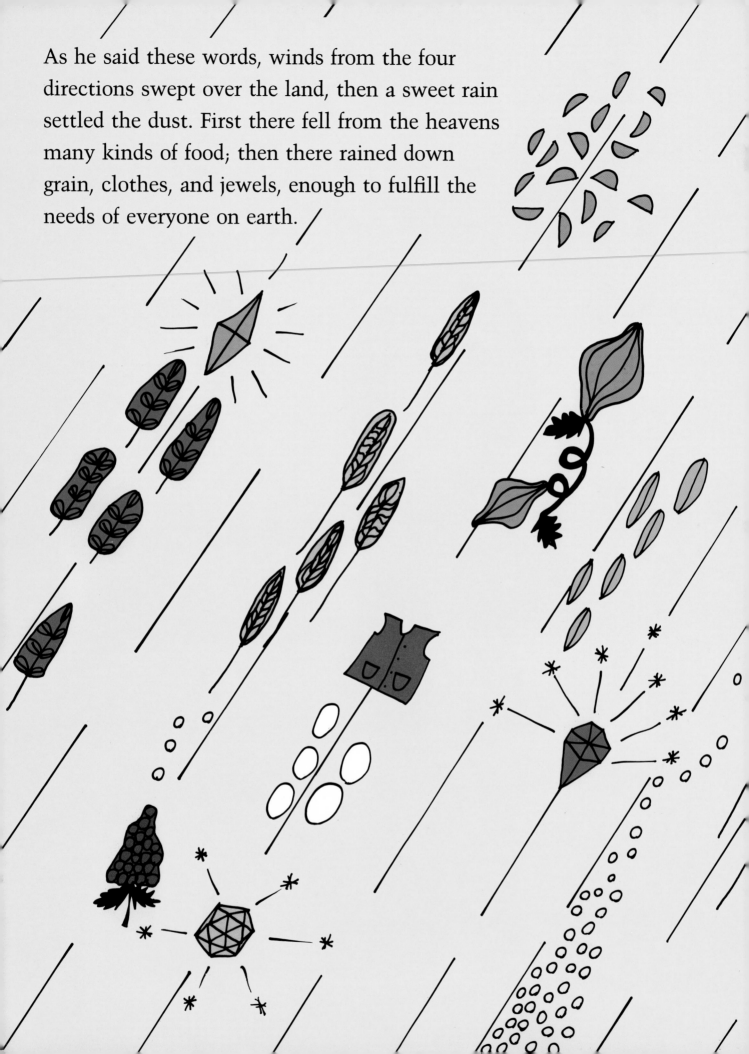

Then a great assembly of people gathered, and Great Gift taught them how to be happy and live together in harmony. Following his teachings, they were kind and generous to each other for the rest of their lives.